FOOD FOR THOUGHT

A collection of heartwarming poetry by
Mrs Yorkshire the Baking Bard

Published by Red Lizard Books
Printed in the UK
Copyright © 2018

About the author

Carol Ellis, who writes under the pen name Mrs Yorkshire the Baking Bard, was born in 1962 in Wakefield, West Yorkshire to Irish parents.

She has been married to Michael since 1985 and they have one daughter, Jessica, born in 1991. She has been living on the Isle of Man since 2007.

She is a performing poet, infamous for her stand up style of comedy in rhyme.

Her poetry has already featured in many local and national newspapers, in magazines and on Channel 5's daytime shows *The Wright Stuff* and *The Jeremy Vine Show.*

She writes observational poetry and her cleverly-crafted poems are both humorous, witty and will have you roaring with laughter.

She also writes poetry to touch the heart and has a talent for bringing very ordinary subjects to life through the rhythmical creation of beauty in words.

Acknowledgements

To my loving husband, Michael. I can always depend on you to support me in anything I do. You give the best advice and have shown me nothing but unconditional love and encouragement.

To my darling daughter, Jessica, the inspiration for my poem *The Empty Nest*. You make me proud every day. My life improved beyond measure the day you were first placed in my arms. You proved there is no bond like the one between mother and child.

To my wonderful mum, who gave me the gift of life. A lovely, nurturing mum from a long line of typical Irish mammies. You have devoted your life to your children and grandchildren and encouraged me to enjoy reading which awakened in me a love of language and writing. The poems I've written for you say it all.

To Chris Payne, who has helped, advised and guided me through the process of publishing. You have enabled me to realise my dream. You made me believe it could happen and made sure it did. I am so grateful for that.

To Graeme Hogg, a wonderfully talented and patient artist. Your illustrations surpassed all my expectations and have helped to bring my poetry to life. I can't thank you enough.

And last, but by no means least, to all my family and friends who have taken the time to read my poetry and watched me perform. Your unfailing support and kind words have given me the confidence to share my poetry.

Illustrated by Graeme Hogg

www.thewholehogg.carbonmade.com

Contents

An Irish Yorkshire Lass

I wrote this poem about my experiences of growing up in Yorkshire during the 1960s and 1970s with Irish parents. I posted this poem on Facebook when I first wrote it and it went viral around the world, indicating how popular the Irish are!

An Irish Yorkshire Lass

When I grew up in Yorkshire I was
carefree, fun and wild
But tales about the banshee petrified me
as a child
I ate bacon, spuds and cabbage and had
barmbrack for my tea
And I listened to the Angelus each night
on RTÉ

Although born in a city, how I longed
for fields of green
Spent my holidays in Mayo where the air
is sweet and clean
With its warm, inviting home fires and
the lovely smell of peat
I wondered why my parents swapped the
earth beneath their feet

I was a crazy mixed up kid I had a
Yorkshire twang
And yet I used the Gaelic words and all
the Irish slang
I went off to the Catholic school where
kids were just the same
Brendan, Kathleen, Mary, Sean and
every Irish name

(Cont...)

I was brought up with pop music – like
Abba, Queen and Wham!
But could belt out a good rebel tune
when I was in my pram
I play the old tin whistle and can sing
The Foggy Dew
And wear shamrock on St Patrick's Day
like all good Paddies do

A splash of holy water kept the
devilment away
I was never short of patron saints to pray
to every day
And when I had a fever I had flat pop
and dry toast
I was chased around for mischief with a
rolled up *Irish Post*

Gatherings with relatives and surely
there were dozens
I joined in well with all the craic, loved
playing with my cousins
A cart load of potatoes and a pan of Irish
stew
Plenty there for all the folks and there
were quite a few

I'm proud my blood is Irish, feel at home
on Irish soil
I've always food for visitors, a kettle on
the boil
I still hold dear my culture but between
both you and me
Instead of drinking Barry's I just love my
Yorkshire Tea!

God's Own County

Anyone who comes from Yorkshire will tell you, 'there's nowt like Yorkshire folk'. My parents emigrated to Yorkshire in the 1950s and, although I have 100% Irish blood, I do feel a great connection to the largest (and arguably the best) county in England. I was born and brought up there and can't help but sing the praises of 'God's own county'.

God's Own County

You can take the lass outta Yorkshire, but
you can't take Yorkshire from 'lass
And for what it's worth, if you're
Yorkshire by birth
You're considered a whole different class

We're regarded exceedingly friendly,
we'll chat to you if you're a stranger
But when we're down south and we open
our mouth
They look at us like we're a danger

Everyone knows that we like what we
say and we say what we bloody well like
And if you're in shock when we're calling
you 'cock'
You'd be minded to just take a hike

We're down-to-earth folk in Yorkshire,
renowned for our good sense of humour
If they say that we're flash and like
spending our cash
Don't believe 'em – it's only a rumour

They say you can tell a Yorkshireman but
you certainly can't tell him much
And if 'our lass' were to spend all his
brass
You can bet he'd be shouting 'how
much?'

(Cont...)

We enjoy a nice Yorkshire pudding it's
compulsory between you and me
If we fancy a cuppa, at dinner or supper
There's only one brew – Yorkshire Tea

There's the world famous Betty's Tea
Rooms where tourists take afternoon tea
They like to be posh and to spend all
their dosh
It's a bit of a mystery to me

They marvel at God's Own County, they
travel through rain, snow and gales
They go for a walk on the walls at York
And a tour of the great Yorkshire Dales

They'll be taking a trip to the seaside, to
Scarborough and Filey no doubt
And when I was a kid, we were happy in
Brid
With a nice bag of chips to take out

Wherever your life may lead you and
wherever you may roam
When at long last, you see Emley Moor
Mast
You know that you're not far from home

Goodbye Hilda

Here's a tribute to my favourite character played by actress Jean Alexander from British TV's longest-running soap, Coronation Street. It received a full-page feature in Inside Soap magazine and is displayed in the green room at the ITV studios for the cast to enjoy.

Goodbye Hilda

On The Street there was Elsie and Ena
and Minnie
Then along came our Hilda with rollers
and pinny
She became a real icon, was true
working class
She could eavesdrop for England, her
voice could break glass

A real tattletale she was constantly
meddling
Gossip and scandal she'd always be
peddling
Her role of town crier she had to uphold
But beneath all the chat lay a true heart
of gold

Her home was her palace where she was
the queen
Her 'muriel' painting a sight to be seen
The infamous three flying ducks on the
wall
The blue mac and headscarf hung up in
the hall

(Cont...)

Her long-suffering hubby was fond of
his liquor
They'd argue and fight and would
constantly bicker
They fought day and night did our Hilda
and Stan
But we all knew she loved him 'cos he
was her man

Jean Alexander brought Hilda to life
The friend and the workmate, the
mother, the wife
Now we hear of her passing there's not a
dry eye
As we sing *Wish me luck as you wave me
goodbye*

Happy Feet

I love to watch amateur productions. I wrote this poem after watching a show performed by the children of a local academy (RSD School of Dance and Performing Arts). The show took my breath away and made me realise just how lucky I am to live on a small island with so many very talented children.

Happy Feet

Last night I went to see a show they
called it Happy Feet
I made my way into the hall and settled
in my seat
The audience was packed with folk from
every generation
I'll tell you now it really was beyond all
expectation

To introduce the evening, a lovely lass
called Shaz
She promised we'd be entertained with
plenty of pizzazz
They'd practised hard, endured late
nights, experienced anxiety
To bring us all a programme packed
with talent and variety

Tiny tots in kitten suits were truly
captivating
Soloists performed for us, their voices
quite breathtaking
Ballroom dancing, hip hop, ballet, Irish,
jazz and tap
We sang along throughout the night and
couldn't help but clap

(Cont...)

A young girl did a monologue, her
acting was spectacular
Chewing gum she spoke in an
American vernacular
Acrobats performed great stunts and
landed in the splits
The whole affair was fabulous and full
of glam and glitz

They even had a harpist, the music was
just splendid
We listened to her mesmerised,
transfixed until it ended
The crowd were all in raptures, you
should have heard them roar
We laughed, we cried and clapped our
hands until they were quite sore

And once the show was over, we left
there on a high
We were sorry that we had to go and
bid them all goodbye
The songs they'd all been singing were
still ringing in my ear
I'm already looking forward to another
show next year

Illegal War

I wrote this poem in response to the Chilcot Inquiry which was published in July 2016 into the British and American invasion of Iraq.

Illegal War

You said there was no other way
It couldn't wait another day
You sent the soldiers off to die
And watched their mothers left to cry

Iraq was ruined, wrecked and smashed
A country left completely trashed
From tyranny to anarchy
A crime against humanity

Ignored the warnings at their cost
Their lives continue to be lost
You said you'd end brutality
But ISIS thrived in savagery

From Save the Children, what a fraud
A global legacy award
Bestowed on you for you to cherish
While there were orphans left to perish

And from this hell and disarray
More terror in the world today
Your war unleashed a dreadful beast
Left carnage in the middle east

(Cont...)

The truth is public Mr Blair
The horror of your lies laid bare
You dared to do this in our name
And won't acknowledge any blame

I'd like to know just how you sleep
When hearing children as they weep
See fathers hold them as they die
And watch their mothers left to cry

Mum

*Everyone has one, and I'm lucky
enough to have a wonderful one. She
has devoted her life to all her children
and grandchildren. She comes from
a long line of typical 'Irish mammies'
who are natural nurturers. There are
some personal references in this poem,
including Silvio's bread shop in Wakefield
and the 'Janet and John' reading books
from the 1960s but, whatever age you are,
you'll definitely relate to this poem.*

33

Mum

You always did your best from the day
that I was born
You held my hand and and kept me safe,
made sure that I was warm
And when I first went out to play and
came back slightly late
You were watching from the window
and waiting at the gate

The other kids went off to school and we
had time to bake
I helped you with the soda bread and
learned to make a cake
You always had your apron on and sang
a song or two
Spancil Hill, Danny Boy and *The Foggy
Dew*

We'd catch the bus and go to town, so
many to be fed
I'd sit on Silvio's windowsill and watch
you choose the bread
My turn came to go to school, you
missed me when I'd gone
It wasn't long until the day another came
along

(Cont...)

I found such joy in writing, and reading
was a thrill
'Janet and John' *Off to Play, High on a
Hill*
Excited I would tell you of each new
book and playmate
And you would always be there waiting
at the school gate

Playing down the fields with friends,
carefree and so lucky
Sliding down the slag heaps and coming
home dead mucky!
Picking blackberries, riding bikes and
fishing with our mates
You were busy scrubbing steps and
painting those front gates

While other mums went off to bingo you
were happy sewing
Working hard to clothe us all as we were
quickly growing
Scrimping, saving, going without so we
had decent shoes
Every penny spent on us, no time for
fags and booze

(Cont...)

The way you made the food go round
was quite a revelation
An Irish mammy always cooking was
your reputation
Father Kelly on his rounds to save each
rogue and sinner
You always made a place for him so he
could stay to dinner!

And when I was much older and I'd go
out at night
You put a hottie in my bed, left on the
outside light
You were watching from the window in
case that I was late
You couldn't go to sleep yourself till I
came through the gate

I left home and married and later had a
daughter
Baked the cakes to songs you sang that I
made sure I taught her
I watched her going off to school, did
not anticipate
That I'd be watching from the window
and waiting at the gate

(Cont...)

She brought such joy, we watched her
grow, she made us really proud
We danced around the kitchen and sung
the songs out loud
One day she'll comfort her own child
and have to stay up late
She'll be watching from the window and
waiting at the gate

The years roll by and time moves on, one
day we'll all be gone
But there'll always be a cake to bake, a
mum to sing a song
She'll wear an apron, just like us and if
her kids are late
She'll be watching from the window and
waiting at the gate

Our NHS

I wrote this poem in 2016 at the height of the junior doctors' dispute in the UK. My first job when I left college was in the National Health Service, and I have many friends and family who work or have worked in this most wonderful institution. I hope that it can be saved for the good of everyone.

Our NHS

Way back in 1948 Nye Bevan had a plan
That healthcare should be free for every
woman, child and man
The NHS was founded – to help the sick
it vowed
The world watched on in envy at a
Britain that was proud

Great advances soon emerged like
vaccines in the fifties
Hip replacements, heart transplants, the
pill came in the sixties
A test tube baby – on the NHS the first
was born
Keyhole surgery, testing DNA became
the norm

But now there's crisis in our own beloved
institution
We look towards our leaders in the hope
of a solution
Instead the junior doctors are devalued
and demoralised
The ones that help to save us are the ones
unfairly demonised

(Cont...)

There's a short supply of midwives, of
nurses and technicians
Healthcare Assistants, Doctors and even
Dietitians
Too few hours in the day, too few days in
the week
With patients waiting for a bed, the
outlook is quite bleak

Never told to take a break as 'tiredness
can kill'
Fourteen hours later and no meal break
taken still
Holding hands of patients as they
breathe their last on earth
Then saving mum and baby in a most
traumatic birth

Seven days a week they work to help the
sick and needy
Unlike our politicians who then dare to
call them greedy
Who do you think will pin your leg or
save your dying child
Or open up your chest to save you on the
roadside?

(Cont...)

MPs enjoy a pay rise and a three month
summer break
They live the high life claiming their
expenses that are fake
Protecting bankers who it seems would
seek to do us harm
Turn a blind eye to their deeds and even
grease their palm

Spin doctors cannot heal us, on them we
can't depend
They're not the dedicated nurse who
soothes us as we mend
The public won't be hoodwinked or
believe their wicked lies
Real doctors are the ones we need, the
ones who save our lives

The Empty Nest

*A personal favourite of mine, written
about my daughter. Whether you're
a mother or not, I'm sure you'll enjoy
it – and if you are a mother, remember
to have your handkerchief at the ready!
(Jessica still has Naughty Teddy who is
mentioned in the poem!)*

The Empty Nest

A child calls for 'mum' when you're out
in the town
And just for a moment you stop and turn
round
But then you remember you're out on
your own
And your own little bird from the nest
has now flown

The kids in the shop run around in the
aisle
Their mums reprimand them, they just
make you smile
That sweet little dress hanging up on the
rack
Makes your heart skip a beat as it takes
you right back

Black patent shoes worn with white frilly
socks
Silk matching ribbons on soft golden
locks
Red velvet dresses with lace petticoats
Cute little hats to match warm winter
coats

(Cont...)

You open the cupboard and silently weep
The baby cup's there that you just had to
keep
As you pull out a tea towel to dry up the
pots
That old baby bib ties your stomach in
knots

The schools are now closed for the long
holiday
And it seems to you like it was just
yesterday
When your garden was full of such
laughter and noise
And the house filled with playmates and
chaos and toys

Falling from scooters and scraping her
knees
Building a den and of course climbing
trees
A child full of mischief shouts down
from a height
Fearless and reckless she gives you a
fright

Rushing inside to take shelter from
showers
Cousins and mates building Lego for
hours
Jackets and shoes all piled up in the hall
Abandoned pushbikes cast aside on the
wall

(Cont...)

Crammed round the table, they're eager to bake
An overcooked biscuit, a lopsided cake
Small sticky fingers try icing a bun
They were such happy days, you recall every one

At the end of the day all tucked up into bed
Freshly washed hair on a warm, sleepy head
That old Naughty Teddy so worn and so battered
Her constant companion so loved and so tattered

Her magical childhood was filled with such joy
She was daring and bold, could outclimb any boy
Artistic and sporty and smart and so funny
The pleasure she brought you could not buy with money

You remember you dreamt of her as you were waking
But there in the real world your heart was just breaking
No head on the pillow, no dolls on the floor
You walk by her bedroom and pause at the door

(Cont...)

The house is so quiet, there's no tots and
mums
No pram in the hallway, no more biscuit
crumbs
What you wouldn't give for a swing on
the grass
To see small fingerprints formed all over
the glass

So cherish each moment, each joy and
each worry
Enjoy every milestone, there's no need
to hurry
Make sure that you treasure each
moment they're young
There's no job more important than
being a mum

The Kindness Revolution

I wrote this in response to the media coverage of the terror attacks that have unfortunately become a part of our lives in recent times. I believe that the pen is mightier than the sword and we can change the world with kind words and good deeds. This was a winning poem in the 2017 Manx Litfest Poetry Trail. Spread the world and let's start a kindness revolution.

The Kindness Revolution

There's a dark and deadly terror that's
spreading round the planet
Alarming tales of hate and fear and acts
that seem Satanic
Reporting in the media fuels panic and
hysteria
Spreading round the globe like some
transmittable bacteria

You can change your profile photo after
every aberration
But ask yourself how does it really
change the situation?
So through this poem I aim to offer
some kind of solution
I'd like to make a change and start a
'kindness revolution'

Let's start with something simple like a
wave, a nod, a smile
Chatting on the bus or train and not on
your mobile
That person sitting next to you is really
not a danger
Every friend you've ever made was once
to you a stranger

(Cont...)

Hindu, Sikh or Atheist, Muslim,
Christian or Jew
These are all your neighbours and they're
just the same as you
Let's end all the hostility, the fear and
segregation
And join all the communities in one big
celebration

Take the time to listen and to learn about
each other
Extend the hand of friendship and be
kind to one another
Invite that person to your home then
look into his face
We have one commonality – it's called
the human race

Teach a child compassion as a part of
education
Tolerance and helpfulness will build a
better nation
An act of kindness every day should be
on the curriculum
Love and understanding will then soon
become the norm to them

I truly think that this behaviour would
become routine
I'm sure it's true that everyone has got a
kindness gene
Let's start the revolution and send this
round the earth
Kindly spread the word and like and
share for all it's worth

Too Young

My friend, Becky, very generously and bravely allowed me to write this poem about her battle with cervical cancer. I wanted this poem to make people stop and think, so I wrote the last line first, as I do with a lot of my poems. This one is for you Becky, your husband John, your family and especially your beautiful daughter Elouise.

Too Young

The letter from the clinic said they'd test
her every quarter
But straight away she found out she was
pregnant with her daughter
They'd do another smear test when the
baby's three months old
But due to the distraction she forgot
what she'd been told

The baby's six months old and so she
books a new appointment
She carries on with motherhood, caught
up in the excitement
A month goes by the test reveals a
further complication
Another test's required to assess the
situation

Sitting in the waiting room, staring at
the walls
Reading endless posters when the
doctor promptly calls
He thinks about his daughter, she's the
centre of his world
He's horrified to think that she's the
same age as this girl

(Cont...)

Cancer of the cervix, it's so absolutely
brutal
An urgent operation for survival would
be crucial
Her world was crashing round her, it was
utterly surreal
All this in a few short months it
somehow seemed unreal

Feeding on her hormones like some
predatory ghoul
Eating at her womanhood so monstrous
and so cruel
Her life held so much promise, she was
filled with such vivacity
The unrelenting horror meant her facing
her mortality

Today is her first Mothers Day, she's had
her operation
She spends the day recovering in quiet
contemplation
She thinks about that carefree girl who
never would have guessed
Her mother saved her life when she
advised that first smear test

(Cont...)

Thinking of what might have been and
what she would have left
Her brother and her parents so
tormented and bereft
To never meet her soulmate and to wake
up to his smile
To never have her daddy proudly walk
her down the aisle

To leave her precious baby and to never
hear her talk
Or not be there to comfort her and never
see her walk
To take her by the hand to school and
hold her when she's weeping
To gently creep into her room and watch
her as she's sleeping

The law dictates a smear test from the
age of twenty five
But if she hadn't had that test she
wouldn't be alive
A shiver runs right through you when
you think what might have been
For when this story first began that girl
was just nineteen...

Memories of Middlestown School

How many of us remember our child's first day at school? All of us, I'm willing to bet.

I lived in a lovely community (Middlestown, Wakefield) and the infant and junior school was very close by.

My daughter started playgroup there aged two-and-a-half, progressed to nursery at three-and-a-half and then went on to the infant and junior school until she left at age 11.

We have such wonderful memories of her time there. I'm still in touch with many of her teachers from that school including a lovely, caring nursery teacher named Rosie Thompson. Her reception class teacher, a wonderful lady called Janet Brook, used a magic wand which she waved when she wanted the class to be quiet – and it worked! My daughter thought her teacher was a real-life fairy and enjoyed every moment in her class. Janet allowed the infamous Naughty Teddy to accompany Jessica to school. She even wrote him a school report at the

the end of the year! Teachers can, and do, make all the difference to children and their parents and we are so thankful for the time Jessica spent at Middlestown School. I wrote this poem just before she left at age eleven and only rediscovered it on a recent trip to my mum's. I was delighted to find that she'd kept a copy!

Memories of Middlestown School

As I sit to write this poem my heart is
filled with joy
When I think of what you've done for
every little girl and boy
When she started nursery my precious
daughter cried
She clung so tightly to my coat and
wouldn't leave my side

As I left my baby, I thought my heart
would break
I bit my lip and fought the tears – I had
to for her sake
You showed her lots of patience and you
chased away her fears
She settled down and had such fun and
soon there were no tears

When she went to 'big school', I knew
that I would miss her
I packed her bag and brushed her hair
and then I went to kiss her
Her ribbons matched her uniform and
she was so delighted
She was nervous and a little scared but
most of all excited

(Cont...)

I live nearby and heard the children
playing through the day
I longed to bring her home but you had
taken her away
No longer did I feel I was the centre of
her world
She was all I'd ever wanted, my precious
little girl

I didn't have to worry as her teacher had
a 'wand'
She thought you were a fairy and you
soon began to bond
She took her Naughty Teddy as he
helped her feel secure
You were there for both of us to help and
reassure

When I watched her concerts I was
waving from the crowd
And now I thought my heart would
burst because I was so proud
You welcomed me to get involved, you
even let me bake
And I have sent my love to you in each
and every cake

I know she has enjoyed her time, her
friends and all her lessons
And now she's grown, she's standing on
the edge of adolescence
We've had such fun and done so much,
the years, oh how they flew
We've cherished every moment of the
time we've spent with you

You're Never Too Old to be Young

I watched a documentary on TV involving an experiment whereby four-year-old children were invited to engage with the residents of an old folks' home. The results were remarkable. I was challenged by a friend who owns old folks' homes on the island to write a poem about it.

You're Never Too Old to be Young

A jaded version of his son, his wrinkles
tell his story
The wispy remnants of her hair, a crown
of faded glory
Trapped behind the walls of age they
watch the world go by
How did the place they live become a
place they go to die?

But when a child climbs on their knee
and takes them by surprise
Instead of watching time they watch the
world through curious eyes
Running, climbing, playing, every
moment filled with wonder
Little hands that weave a spell they
willingly fall under

The patter of their tiny feet that echo
through the halls
Laughter like their fingerprints
imprinted on the walls
Creaking bones rise from a chair,
emboldened to take part
Dancing to the beat of an enchanted
infant's heart

(Cont...)

No longer playing serious, they seriously
play
Captivating children, reading fairy tales
each day
The old and wise that teach the young so
eager to find out
And yet these children teach them what
life's really all about

Resting weary bones each night they
drift off with a smile
Contented in the knowledge that their
days are still worthwhile
They've helped to put the smile into a
sleeping cherub's eye
The place they live's no longer just a
place they go to die...

Freedom

*I wrote the following poem to celebrate
National Poetry Day in 2017. Each
year there's a different theme and that
particular year's theme was Freedom.
It made me think about what freedom
meant to me and this is what I came up
with.*

Freedom

Let go of what you can't control and set
your spirit free
Refuse to let your fellow man define who
you can be
Don't be content to join the crowd and
thus become a clone
Allow yourself the freedom to be proud
and stand alone

Don't stab your rival in the back if he
should cause you strife
Instead take up the cord and gently cut it
with the knife
Embrace the chance to walk away and
prove you didn't need him
Forgiveness and indifference will guide
the path to freedom

So be yourself and no-one else whatever
should prevail
You alone can play that role at which you
cannot fail
Freedom is a choice and you can choose
to free your mind
Only you can build the walls in which
you are confined

My Mum's Kitchen

This one's a real 'feelgood' poem. My mum's kitchen is a place that's been filled with so many family, friends and memories over the years. Whenever I think of my mum I invariably think of her in the kitchen. Whenever I go back to my childhood home she's always there waiting for me in the kitchen – with the kettle on the boil and food in the oven!

My Mum's Kitchen

Returning from school at the end of the
day
All rosy red cheeks from a long day at
play
I'd run down the path, through the old
kitchen door
And sit down at the table as often before

Hearty roast dinners and hot Irish stew
Warm apple pie and a freshly made brew
Crammed round a table where siblings
would fight
Over who'd had the most of the *Angel
Delight*

She'd live in the kitchen for most of the
day
Mum would be singing whilst working
away
Clearing away once the meals had all
ended
With jumpers to knit and our clothes to
be mended

Sitting high on the worktop when I was
so small
Comforting me from a scrape or a fall
Wiped the tears on her apron then back
out to play
Had a bath in the sink at the end of the
day!

(Cont...)

As a teen in the morning the radio was
on
And we'd hear Noel Edmonds on Radio
One
Eating toast on the step with the door
open wide
Watching out for the school bus to pull
up outside

There was always a welcome should
visitors call
Whether family or friends there'd be
plenty for all
And as we grew older at each celebration
We had to make room for the next
generation

They say that the kitchen's the heart of
the home
And you'll always end up there wherever
you roam
No posh lavish restaurants and fancy
hotels
Can compare to that kitchen's most
heavenly smells

The decades have passed and we've all
flown the nest
But she's still in the kitchen, the place I
love best
I feel so at home as I walk through the
door
And sit down at that same kitchen table
once more

Different Worlds

I wrote this poem to celebrate World Poetry Day 2018. The theme was 'The World', so I challenged myself to write a poem using the word 'world' in every line.

Different Worlds

'It's a funny old world' ain't that the truth
'The world's your oyster' we're telling our
youth
There's a 'brave new world' now they're
coming of age
In the era of Facebook 'all the world's a
stage'

The 'world wide web' is the new fixation
Made 'a world of difference' to a
generation
You're all 'world famous' and sharing
your life
Baring your soul for 'the world and his
wife'

But 'a world apart' in a far-off nation
A 'third world country' enduring
starvation
In the 'modern world' how do you
explain?
The human race in 'a world of pain'

Be Kind

*Finally, as this book of poetry is designed
to 'touch the heart', I shall finish with
a poem I wrote with a positive and
heartwarming message. There is no
better time than now to be kind. This was
a winning poem in the Manx Litfest 2018
Poetry Trail.*

Be Kind

See the good in others and find
goodness in your heart
Don't allow maliciousness to tear your
soul apart
Be the voice of reason in a disapproving
crowd
Rise above distrust and be the rainbow
in a cloud

Plant a seed of kindness and then gently
watch it flower
Embrace the power of love and disregard
the love of power
Set aside your pain and have the courage
to forgive
It doesn't matter what you have, it
matters what you give

Compassion is a frame of mind that
everyone can learn
Show mankind goodwill expecting
nothing in return
Judging other people will define just
who *you* are
Choose your words with kindness –
leave a mark and not a scar

(Cont...)

So in this world of building walls
let's build a bridge instead
And walk across to free the world of
anguish, fear and dread
Making peace with others serves to give
us peace of mind
Be gentle and be tolerant, above all just
be kind

The Rhyme of My Life: The story of Mrs Yorkshire the Baking Bard

Night Mail poem

So when did all this 'poetry malarkey' begin? Well, when I was in the second year of high school we read a poem by W H Auden, *Night Mail*. You may be familiar with the poem.

At the time there were problems with the roof of our high school so the first and second year pupils were re-located to a disused Victorian school near the city centre. The classrooms had large windows which were located above head height, preventing children

Ings Road School, Wakefield

from daydreaming out of the window or being distracted by the world outside. It was a late afternoon lesson and by now my thoughts were turning to catching the bus home with friends. Beams of sun boldly streamed into the room and I watched the dust particles dancing within them, willing the time to pass.

Our English teacher began reading the poem and suddenly I was transfixed. The rhythm of the poem conjured up the image of the train bustling through the British night-time countryside. I wanted to be able to write poetry like that. I'd read books and pieces of prose but this was something else. This was like dancing instead of walking.

The ability to connect with someone, anyone, whether friends or strangers, through the power of words, both fascinated and thrilled me in equal measure.

In that moment I realised that through the use of language in all its beauty and different forms, I could reach into the hearts and minds of people and make them laugh, cry, contemplate, examine, reflect and ultimately share my passion for the words and their message.

Our homework was set – to write a poem in the same style. A train journey, any train journey of our choice. I could see my classmates were packing their books away. To them it was just the end of another boring lesson. I felt detached from my surroundings. My mind was racing. I was already thinking about what I was going to write.

I queued up for the school bus. I was the chatterbox of the group and often led the conversation which usually revolved around pop music, fashion, a TV programme or techniques implemented to achieve the latest hairstyle, but I was still distracted. Words and rhymes were already running around my head in anticipation of writing my poem.

I ran into the house and as usual we gathered round the table for our tea. It was a busy, noisy house. Four children and two adults. There was always plenty of activity. People coming and going. The constant clatter of pots and pans from the kitchen. Radio Eireann blasting out Irish music, my mum singing along and my father occasionally playing his tin whistle. There were the usual altercations, raised voices and doors slamming.

I shared a bedroom with my older sister but fortunately this evening she was otherwise engaged watching TV downstairs, which was just as well because there was an unwritten rule that being the oldest she was in charge. It was primarily her bedroom. Most evenings the whole family would huddle round the fire in the living room to watch TV as there was no central heating in the house. Some evenings I braved the cold in my bedroom to listen to Radio Luxembourg on a transistor radio, a pop music station which broadcasted on 208 medium wave every evening during the 1970s. The DJ, Tony Prince, or my favourite, 'Kid' Jensen, would host *The Battle of the Bands* – the *Bay City Rollers vs The Osmonds* or *David Cassidy vs David Essex*. My sister sometimes listened with me.

If I had enough pocket money I'd buy the *Fabulous 208* magazine which listed the song lyrics of all my favourite artists of the day. I'd carefully remove the staples from the centre pages and place the full colour poster spread across the middle pages on the wall above my bed.

I relished the fact that I had the bedroom to myself and wasted no time in retrieving my English homework book from my school bag which I'd thrown hastily on the bed. I had to kneel on the floor against the bed, my legs tucked underneath me, using the bed as a makeshift desk. The candlewick bedspread against my body and legs kept me warm and I'd closed the door to block out the noise from the rest of the family downstairs. I remembered the poem by Auden. As the teacher read it aloud I'd heard the underlying rhythm, mimicking the sound of a train on the tracks.

I began writing and found the ability to use the correct amount of stressed and unstressed syllables in each line came easily to me, as though I was singing a song. Once I started writing it was a like a tap had been turned on in my head. The words came flowing out, spilling onto the page. An exhilarating journey of creativity and self-discovery.

I was pleased with my efforts and duly handed my homework in. A couple of days later at the beginning of the lesson the English teacher moved around the room, skilfully dodging the school bags carelessly discarded on the floor, as if negotiating an army assault course. He shouted out each pupil's mark as he handed back their homework. Sometimes he paused and made comments: 'good effort', 'watch your spelling'. I waited impatiently for my homework to be returned until he only had one book left in his hand.

As he returned to his desk a wave of panic rose within me. Had I misunderstood the instructions and written something completely different to everyone else? A sudden rush of heat enveloped me and I sat up straight in my chair, arms folded in front of me as if to protect myself from the inevitable onslaught of humiliation and mortification.

After what seemed like an age he held my book up and proceeded to inform the class that he wanted to read my poem to everyone as an example of the correct interpretation of the homework set! He was very impressed by my use of metre and rhyme. He told the class to listen to the rhythm as he read.

My face still burned like a hot pan on a stove, the anticipation of hearing my poem read aloud bubbling inside me. An extraordinary sense of elation swept over me as I listened to him read the poem, just as I'd intended it to be read. I could hear the rhythm of the train – my train, not the train with the *Night Mail,* but the one I'd envisaged rattling along the tracks through verdant countryside on a warm summer's day.

I felt dizzy with delight. I wanted to close my eyes and savour the moment. All eyes were upon me. There were audible gasps and murmurs of appreciation. The ball in my throat threatened to escape my lips. I burned with a fierce joy.

That was just the beginning of my love affair with language and words. Whenever the teacher asked us to write a story for homework, I became completely engrossed. Nothing else was important. During the subsequent lessons I became distracted. My mind was like a butterfly fluttering back to the story I'd already started writing in my head.

By the time I reached the fourth year I had a different but no less encouraging English teacher. His name was Mr Devlin. He always read my stories to the class. I think he appreciated my enthusiasm, even though I was a 'lively' member of the class, partial to a fair amount of giggling and chattering.

Age 16, centre of photo

One day, as we were filing past his desk to go to the next lesson, he stopped me and told me I had a gift and I musn't waste it. A gift? What did that mean to a 15-year-

old girl, and what did he mean that I musn't waste it? OK so I could write a good story, tell a good tale, but I put that down to my Irish upbringing. I was from a working class family and shouldn't get ideas above

St Thomas à Becket School

my station. I'd leave school, maybe go to college, get a job, meet a nice young man, get married and start a family.

And that's exactly what I did. I left school, went to secretarial college, got a job, met a nice young man, got married and had a daughter. I still read books when I had the time. Occasionally, if someone was leaving work or having a special birthday, I wrote a poem. I didn't even bother to keep copies.

Once I became a mother it was all-consuming. I wanted to recreate *The Little House on the Prairie*. To be the perfect wife and mother. To indulge my child with my time and make her childhood as magical as possible. To be an accomplished housekeeper and cook. 'She always keeps a good table'. That's what I used to hear when I was growing up.

Eventually my husband, Michael and I,

together with our daughter, Jessica, re-located from Yorkshire to live on the Isle of Man.

Maughold Village, Isle of Man

A couple of years later Jessica went across the sea to Queen's University in Belfast and suddenly there was just the two of us. I was in my late forties. She left university, got a job and settled in the north of Ireland. We had an empty nest and our thoughts turned to slowing down and not working so many hours.

We were running our small mail order company together when my husband returned to working in advertising. We scaled the mail order company down and essentially I was working part time.

At the top of Maughold Head

I missed my daughter terribly and felt it would be a good distraction to indulge myself a little. I started walking for pleasure and fitness. I baked cakes for friends and family. Whatever the occasion I'd turn up with a cake!

I was sitting down one day, my thoughts turning to life on the Isle of Man and all its quirks and curiosities. We would have been living here nine years in just over a month. I started to write, not with

Selling my cupcakes

83

a pen but with a keyboard. My fingers danced skilfully across the keys as ideas popped into my head. It was like an epiphany, I could write a poem to celebrate because I could write poetry! Of course I could write poetry, I used to write poetry, why hadn't I written poetry for so long?

I read the poem to my husband. He thought it was very good. Would he have dared tell me if it was rubbish? I wasn't too sure. My friend Sonia came round. She's a straight talking Geordie lass. Kind but honest. She listened intently and when I'd finished she said it was brilliant. She encouraged me to post it on Facebook.

I still wasn't convinced and read it to a couple of other people who were similarly impressed. Sonia beseeched me to post the poem on Facebook so that others could enjoy and appreciate it, particularly our friends on the island. After much deliberation, a month later, on the ninth anniversary of moving here, I took the plunge and posted the poem on my Facebook page.

I was like that 13-year-old girl again, filled with uncertainty and anticipation. However, within minutes the poem was being commented on favourably and shared all over Facebook. Of course, I still doubted myself: after all, these were my friends. They wouldn't be cruel enough to criticise the composition I'd carefully created and crafted for their enjoyment. I wrote a couple more poems and these too were received very positively.

A few months later I joined the Isle of Man Poetry Society. I hadn't even realised there was one except a friend told me about it. I went along to the meeting with only three poems in my folder.

A group of people were sitting around a large table. Each member read a poem to the group, either one that they'd written or one from a book. I began to think I'd probably made a mistake as the poetry didn't appear to be in the same vein as mine. Oh dear, what would they make of my poetry? There was to be a break for coffee half-way through and I considered leaving quietly through the back door.

Just before we broke for coffee a gentleman began reading one of his own compositions. As he began reading I felt relief wash over me. His poetry was a very similar style to mine.

The chairperson asked if I had anything I'd like to read so I nervously retrieved my poem about the Isle of Man from my folder and began to read. It's a humorous and affectionate poem entitled *The Come Over.*

They appeared to be laughing in all the correct places. I finished and held my breath. Everyone clapped. Thank goodness – I hadn't offended anyone and they actually appeared to enjoy my poetry.

We had coffee and I chatted to the gentleman who read before me. He was there with his wife, also a talented poet.

It transpired that he was something of a local celebrity. He wrote a column in the Manx Independent, the island's main newspaper, and featured on local radio once a week. Indeed, much like Cher, Cilla and Lulu, he was known by only one name: 'Pullyman'. I felt I was in the presence of some rather special people.

In the second half of the meeting another gentleman began reading his own poetry. This blew my mind. He appeared to have an encyclopaedic knowledge of rhyming and metre schemes and this was reflected in his poetry which was both witty and superbly written.

After the meeting the gentleman, whose name is Dennis Turner, approached me and asked if he could discuss my poetry with me as he enjoyed it very much. His words were 'I think you've got something'.

I met with Dennis and we chatted over my homemade cake and a cup of Yorkshire Tea. He spoke to me about my use of 'feminine endings'. I didn't even know there was such a thing but apparently I was using these to great effect!

I felt honoured that he was imparting his knowledge to me. He said he couldn't really teach me anything as I instinctively followed the rules of good metre and rhyme but he wanted me to know why I was doing what I did.

I was like a child, hungry for knowledge and eager to learn. He began talking about iambic, trochaic, spondaic and dactylic metres. He explained the use of stressed and unstressed syllables. I vaguely remembered some of it from school. Poetry became increasingly fascinating.

I know his in-depth knowledge of metre and rhyme which he has so generously shared with me and continues to do so, inspires me to this day and has improved my writing beyond measure.

Through the Poetry Society meetings I discovered the poetry Open Mic events which take place on the island. These are organised by another very talented poet called Hazel Teare. Hazel also comperes these evenings.

Performing with IOM poets

I'd enjoyed amateur dramatics at school and quite often took the lead role in school productions. Maybe this was because I had a loud voice, but either way I figured this would come in handy at the Open Mic events and for performing in public!

Performing as a witch, age 15

The Open Mic events have grown in such popularity that spectators are regularly turned away as they're full to capacity. They've also given me the opportunity to hone my performance skills considerably.

Hazel started the Open Mic evenings a few years before to give anyone wishing to perform their poetry a platform. It was a kind of rebellion against the stuffy academic image poetry

Performing at Manx Litfest

has and the idea that only academics can successfully produce good poetry. Making poetry accessible to all is the key to their success.

Once I became involved with the poetry scene on the island I soon began performing at local charity events and private functions. I tailor my poetry to suit the audience and find the more I perform the easier it becomes.

Performing at the Isle of Man Hospice 35th Anniversary event for volunteers, Douglas

I decided to create a public Facebook page to share my poetry and that's when I came up with the idea for a pen name. Since living on the island I've become known as *Mrs Yorkshire* as I'm instantly recognisable by my accent. I'm also well-known for my baking skills so I put the two together and came up with *Mrs Yorkshire the Baking Bard.*

The page enabled me to connect with poetry lovers from all over the world. As I write observational poetry on all subjects, I've been able to share poems of specific interest to certain groups and attract more followers.

On special occasions I share relevant poetry. At Christmas I share my poem *Carol for Christmas*. On Valentine's Day I share my poem *A Yorkshire Valentine* and, of course, I always share my *Halloween* poem on 31st October. During the year there are many other special days such as St Patrick's Day, Yorkshire Day, Breast Cancer Awareness month – the list is endless.

Facebook: Mrs Yorkshire the Baking Bard

I also began writing poetry with certain days in mind. On National Poetry Day a couple of years ago I wrote a poem and posted it to Channel 5's daytime TV show *The Wright Stuff*. I was stunned when they actually read it out live on air.

I wrote a poem to celebrate International Women's Day and this time Matthew Wright, the presenter of the show, contacted me and asked me if I'd like to video the poem so that I could read it myself on the show! I was absolutely delighted and duly did so.

The Wright Stuff

A few months later it was announced he was leaving the show after eighteen years.

I was so grateful for his kindness that I sent him good wishes and wrote a few lines in verse to wish him well.

The Wright Stuff

Matthew contacted me again and asked if I'd be kind enough to video the poem to feature on his final show. I was honoured and delighted to do this. I've since appeared on *The Jeremy Vine Show,* which replaced *The Wright Stuff,* reading a poem for National Poetry Day again.

I've also had my poems published in many local and national newspapers and magazines.

My husband, Michael, convinced me that I should set up a Youtube channel so I've made videos of a few of my poems and uploaded them onto there too. Go to youtube.com and type in 'Mrs Yorkshire' to view the videos on my channel.

During this time a very good friend of ours came to visit us on the island. Chris Payne is a very successful and highly respected businessman who began his career in marketing in the 1980s. He has worked as a reviews editor, mainly for computer magazines, and created Europe's largest mail order supplier of light and sound machines including lucid dreaming machines and other devices. He's currently the Managing Director of Effort-Free

Media Ltd, helping consultants, trainers and coaches to create quality e-products they can give away and sell.

Chris had been reading my poetry online and watching my videos on my Youtube channel. He encouraged me to publish my poetry. I told him it was a dream of mine to publish a book and he convinced me that, with his help, it would happen. He advised me to write a trilogy of books, each of the three books on a different theme, and suggested that each poem should have an illustration to accompany it.

I was lucky enough to find a very talented, experienced and highly respected artist and illustrator, Graeme Hogg at *The Whole Hogg*. His illustrations have brought my poetry to life. I never even considered illustrating the books but I'm so pleased I did. You can have a look at more of Graeme's work on his web site https://thewholehogg.carbonmade.com/. You won't be disappointed.

So, after not even three years of re-discovering my love of poetry, here I am publishing a trilogy of poetry books. I'm 56 years old and have realised it's never too late to follow your dreams and make them come true. I've had a lot of support and encouragement and made lots of friends along the way.

My books are available to purchase

separately or as a trilogy at a reduced price. If you've purchased any of my books from Amazon, please leave me feedback in the reviews. It's great to connect with my readers.

I'm always open to requests to write on any subject, so if you think there's something I should write about, drop me a line and tell me!

You can write to me at c/o Red Lizard Ltd, PO Box 18, Ramsey, Isle of Man, British Isles, IM99 4PG, e-mail me at carolellis2012@gmail.com, or message me through my Facebook page: *Mrs Yorkshire the Baking Bard.*

I'm happy to post signed copies of books. I accept commissions to write poetry to order. If you have a specific event or celebration, as long as I have a few details regarding the person you'd like the poem for, I can come up with something especially for them. I'm also happy to perform at corporate and charity events, social functions and engage in TV and radio appearances.

I have a book stuffed full of ideas for poems, all waiting to be written. If there were more hours in the day I could fill them writing poetry. I know I'll never run out of things to write about if I live to be over 100 years old!

Thank you for reading my poetry. My original dream as a 13-year-old girl was to share my love of words with the world and, finally, I believe that dream has come true.

Carol Ellis
Mrs Yorkshire the Baking Bard
X

Also available

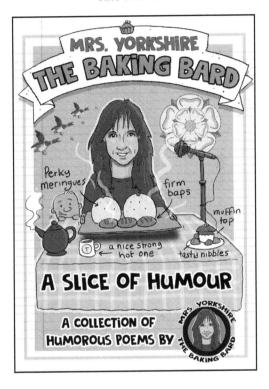

Mrs Yorkshire the Baking Bard
c/o Red Lizard Ltd
PO Box 18
Ramsey
Isle of Man
IM99 4PG

carolellis2012@gmail.com

Facebook: Mrs Yorkshire the Baking Bard

YouTube: Mrs Yorkshire the Baking Bard

Give it a Go

Why not have a go at writing your own
poetry? I believe you can write a poem
about any subject. Write down a few ideas
about what you'd like to say about your
subject matter and let each idea form a
verse.

If you're stuck for a rhyme, use the
Rhymezone web site, it's far more useful
than going through the alphabet in your
head, chanting rhyming words!

As you've probably gathered, I like
to write rhyming poetry with good,
structured metre. Metre is the basic
rhythmic structure of a verse or lines in a
poem. I find poetry with structured metre
much easier to recite and much easier for
the reader to read too. If you're in doubt
about whether a line 'scans', even after
you've read it back, count the number of
syllables in each line to see if they match.
You may need to swap one word for
another so that it fits. A Thesaurus is very
useful for this. There is a web site called
Thesaurus to make it easier for you.

I've left a few blank pages at the back of
this book for you to write down your
ideas and, who knows, you may release
your inner poet. Go on, give it a go. You
may find you enjoy writing poetry as

much as reading it.

Why not write a poem about something
we can all relate to? You can make
it humorous, sentimental, thought-
provoking – the possibilities are endless.
Overleaf I've written the first couple of
lines of the poem to start you off. Keep
your verses to four lines each in rhyming
couplets. Good luck!

Mrs Yorkshire the Baking Bard x

Here are the first two lines of a poem to inspire you to write the rest. Good luck!

Music

Music is a masterpiece, harmonic work of art
Can heal the soul, and clear the mind, can mend a broken heart

Printed in Poland
by Amazon Fulfillment
Poland Sp. z o.o., Wrocław